Virtual Friends Again

by

Mary Hoffman

Illustrated by Shaun McLaren

D1646854

You do not need to read this page – just get on with the book!

First published in 2001 in Great Britain by
Barrington Stoke Ltd
www.barringtonstoke.co.uk

Reprinted 2001, 2002, 2003, 2004, 2005

ISBN 1-902260-82-1

Printed in Great Britain by Bell and Bain Ltd

Meet The Author - MARY HOFFMAN

What is your favourite animal?
Any kind of cat
What is your favourite boy's name?
Lorenzo
What is your favourite girl's name?
Arianwen
What is your favourite food?
Indian

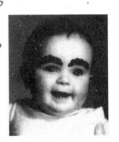

What is your favourite music?
Opera - especially Wagner and Mozart
What is your favourite hobby?
Reading and swimming - but not at the same time!

Meet The Illustrator - SHAUN MCLAREN

What is your favourite animal?
A gnu
What is your favourite boy's name?
Joe
What is your favourite girl's name?
Joyce (my wife)
What is your favourite food?
Peanut butter and banana sandwiches
What is your favourite music?
A bit of everything!
What is your favourite hobby?
Balancing things on the end of my pencil

For all the consultants who read and liked this book – their names are at the back of the book!

Contents

Chapter 1
Mister VR

"You'll be coming with me, won't you?" asked Dad, as he waved a piece of paper under Ben's nose. It was a flyer advertising the opening of a new shop in the High Street. "It would mean a lot to Vince if you were there."

"Where?" asked Ben, grabbing the flyer, though he had a horrible idea he knew the answer.

Vince Riggs was their next-door neighbour. He was a friendly bear of a man, who was nuts about computers and virtual reality games. You might think this made him great fun as a neighbour, but this was only partly true. He had got them all into trouble in the past.

Vince used to keep all his computer stuff in a HUGE wooden shed that took up all the space in his back garden.

One day, his wife Sylvia had finally put her foot down. She had always wanted a proper garden with a lawn for Vince to mow, just like all the other houses in Belmont Avenue, where they lived.

The last straw for Sylvia had been the day that the electricity had been cut off because Vince had forgotten to pay the bill. She had moved in with her sister and for a whole week Vince had come and had all his dinners with Ben and Ben's Dad, who worked with computers himself.

But that wasn't why Ben had been avoiding Vince. It was what else had happened the day the electrics went down.

Ben had been playing a virtual reality game in Vince's shed that Saturday when the electricity was cut off. He had used a computer program to design a perfect friend for himself. He had called him 'Rory Polestar' and had had a great time with him. Rory had disappeared when the power went off. That was not surprising. What was astonishing was that Rory had turned up at Ben's school on Monday morning!

Rory and Ben had had a fantastic week together. Everyone seemed to want to be where Rory was. Ben made lots of new friends. But the day the electricity had come back on again, Rory had faded and disappeared.

Ever since, Ben hadn't known what to think about Rory, so he tried not to think about him at all. That's why he avoided Vince. It brought it all back.

Now it looked as if Ben couldn't avoid Vince any longer. "I don't know if I can come, Dad," Ben said now, trying to wriggle out of it. "I've got a lot of homework."

"Since when have you done your homework on a Saturday afternoon?" asked Dad. "There's plenty of time the rest of the weekend. Go on – I've told Vince we'll be there."

Ben sighed and looked at the flyer again.

GRAND OPENING!

The only virtual reality studio in South Hanbury is opening at:

166 High Street

THIS SATURDAY AFTERNOON AT 2pm!!

Don't miss this chance to sample another universe at half-price if you bring this flyer!

Destinations unlimited!

The Caribbean, Atlantis, King Arthur's Court, Dinosaur World, Outer Space - you choose!

Vince Riggs, Mr VIRTUAL REALITY himself
CAN TAKE YOU THERE!
See you Saturday!

BE THERE OR BE NOWHERE!!

"I'd rather be nowhere," muttered Ben under his breath, but he could see that Dad had made up his mind.

****

Next morning at school, Dylan came straight over to Ben. With him as usual were Assad, Kieran and Gerry, the only girl in the group.

"You coming to Mister VR's tomorrow?" was the first thing Dylan said to Ben.

"I suppose so," said Ben. He saw that Dylan and all his other friends were holding Vince's flyers and looking pretty excited. Ben would have been excited too, normally, but he still felt uneasy about Rory. No-one ever talked about him, for one thing. The name of Rory Polestar was never mentioned.

And yet Dylan, Gerry and the others had been crazy about him.

Rory, with his dreadlocks and his big grin and his wicked sense of fun, had been the most popular kid in the school. And then he had just been wiped out, like the writing on yesterday's whiteboard.

Ben tried over lunch. "Dylan," he began, "you know when I first came here, last term?"

"Yes," said Dylan, munching on a chip. "You were a right wimp."

They stopped eating for a bit to exchange friendly thumps.

"Anyway, what about it?" continued Dylan, picking up another chip.

"Well, you know I came late, after the start of term and I didn't have any friends?"

"Yeah," said Dylan.

"Do you remember why that changed and why you and Gerry and Assad and Kieran all started to be my friends?" asked Ben.

Dylan frowned. "We found out you were into the same things, like skating, that's all."

"Do you remember my friend Rory?" asked Ben, his heart beating loudly.

Dylan looked at first as if he did remember, then he shook his head. "Sorry. Was he at your old school?"

Ben gave up. "Something like that," he said.

****

Saturday dawned cold and wet. But the rain was not an excuse for getting out of Vince's Grand Opening. The High Street was only a couple of streets away and if it was wet, that was all the more reason to play virtual reality games indoors.

Ben's Dad wasn't the sort who would ever say, "You ought to be out enjoying the fresh air on a lovely day like this, not frowsting indoors over a computer screen."

Dad was the sort of person who preferred computer screens to running about in the fresh air any day of the week. Ben's Mum might have said it, but she had died over two years ago.

After breakfast, Ben discovered that things were even worse than he had thought. They weren't just going to Vince's Grand Opening – Dad had volunteered their services

to help him get the studio ready in the morning.

"Hurry up, Ben," he said, as soon as Ben had finished his third piece of toast. "I told Vince we'd be there by ten."

Ben found the studio was a lot better than he had been expecting. The shopfront was newly-painted in purple and silver, with 'Mister VR' written inside a huge pair of goggles over the door.

The plate glass window was painted white on the inside, to hide the contents from passers-by.

Vince was in the doorway looking out for them and let them in. "Ta-ra!" he said dramatically, flinging out his arms and inviting them to admire the set-up.

Ben remembered being impressed by the banks of computer screens even when they were in Vince's old shed, but here on the High Street, they looked even better.

"All right, eh, Ben?" asked Vince, reading his thoughts. "Better than the shed?"

"Yeah, it looks really good," said Ben. "Have you got any new programs?"

"Have I ever," said Vince, rubbing his hands with glee. "Tell you what, Ben. You finish putting the prices on the programs and your Dad can help me set up the sound system for this afternoon. There should be time for you to try one before the opening."

Ben spent quite an interesting morning looking through the new stock and doing odd jobs for Vince.

At one o'clock Vince brought in some fish and chips and they ate them off the reception desk. "Why don't you have a go on one of the computers, Ben?" asked Vince, when they had finished. "There's nothing left to do except the refreshments and Sylvia's bringing them, so you can relax."

Ben chose a new program, one for a virtual reality bungee jump and went to plug it into one of the computers.

He put on his helmet and gloves and looked at his personal screen. He hesitated, then took the helmet off again and took out another program. It was the old 'Virtual Friend' one, which Ben had found in Vince's stockroom when he was sticking on price labels. He looked over his shoulder and saw that Vince and Dad were busy helping Sylvia to carry in the boxes of crisps and squash.

Ben opened up the program and found that there were still some saved options. And there were the magic words – RORY POLESTAR! Ben's heart was beating fast as he put the helmet and gloves back on and started up the program. He saw the familiar settings and this time chose MOONSCAPE. He pressed the GO button and waited.

At once, he felt weightless. He looked down at his feet in their huge moonboots and took a few big, bouncing steps. He was in a grey, rocky, dusty place. In front of him there were craters, behind him a big, white spaceship. Suddenly the door of the ship opened and another astronaut came slowly down the steps.

Even through the big goldfish bowl helmet, Ben could see the startled face of the best friend he had ever had, the one he had designed for himself – Rory Polestar.

Chapter 2
The Grand Opening

"Hey, Bendigo!" said Rory, grinning at Ben through his helmet. "How you doin'?" Then a puzzled expression crossed his face. "This is a dream, right? I mean – we're on the moon, man!"

Ben didn't know where to begin. He was so pleased to see Rory again, but how could he explain what was happening? He was beginning to wish he hadn't chosen the moon option. It was difficult to talk with helmets on and the way they were bouncing up and down was distracting.

"Hey, Rory," Ben said nervously. "There's something I've got to try to explain to you. You remember the first time we met, in the park?"

Rory frowned. "I guess so. But it seemed as if we'd known each other before."

"The thing is ..." said Ben. "This is going to sound ridiculous, but I ... I sort of invented you."

Rory bounced gently, flexing his knees. "OK, this is definitely a dream. How could you have invented me? I've been alive for twelve years."

"I know it sounds crazy," said Ben. "Maybe I only *thought* I invented you.

Maybe I just sort of transported you from wherever you were."

"I was in the park," said Rory. "*You* were the one who appeared out of nowhere."

Ben sighed. "I know. I was in a virtual reality program, trying to make a friend. I chose the park and then there you were."

"But what about when we were in school?" asked Rory.

"You remember that?" said Ben eagerly.

"Of course," said Rory, but then he hesitated. "Man, I don't know. That was all a bit like a dream too. My Mum said I'd skived off school for a week, but I remember being there with you and Dylan and the others."

Ben wondered how on earth he could explain something that he didn't understand himself.

"Rory, why do you think we're on the moon now?"

"Because I had too much chilli in my dinner and I'm having a really weird dream," said Rory promptly.

"No," said Ben firmly. "I'm in a virtual reality studio. I chose the MOONSCAPE setting and I programmed you into it."

"Prove it," said Rory, spreading his hands.

"OK," said Ben slowly. "I'll shut down the program, then I'll choose a new setting. Will you believe me if you next meet me in, say, the coffee shop?"

Rory looked as if he was interested, but Ben never knew what he might have said, because at that moment his helmet was wrenched off.

"Hey!" said Dylan, holding Ben's helmet. "That's cheating. You're having a go before the Grand Opening!"

Ben blinked in the bright lights of Mister VR's. More than half his brain was still on the silent, grey moon with Rory. The sudden noise and glare made him feel stupid. The studio was full of excited kids and parents. Vince was beaming with happiness. He was about to cut a big, purple ribbon that Sylvia had fixed in front of the virtual reality units. Ben was on the wrong side of the ribbon and Dylan was leaning over it and grinning at him.

"Come out of it, Ben," said Dad. "Vince wants to cut the ribbon and open up."

Ben just had time to slip the Virtual Friend program into his pocket. Then he had to do a limbo shuffle under the ribbon to join his friends.

"Your attention, Ladies and Gentlemen," said Vince, waving his scissors. "It gives me great pleasure to welcome you to the opening of Mister VR's. That's me, Mister Virtual Reality, Vince Riggs. I hope you have a wonderful time. My lovely wife, Sylvia will book you in and take your money – don't forget it's half-price with one of my flyers. And while you're waiting please help yourselves to refreshments. I now declare the Virtual Reality studio well and truly OPEN!"

Everyone clapped and then rushed to the reception desk, where Sylvia was soon overwhelmed by people waving flyers. And that was that, as far as Ben was concerned. He knew he wouldn't be able to get back to the Virtual Friend program for the rest of the afternoon.

Vince and Dad had him running around, pouring out more squash and cola, collecting empty cups, even counting money and putting it into little, plastic bags. There were lots of virtual reality units but the queues to get on them were huge because lots of people wanted to use them.

When the studio closed at seven o'clock, Ben and Dad, Vince and Sylvia were all worn out.

But Vince was excited too. He had made a lot of money and was sure he was going to make a lot more, once word got around. "There'll be birthday parties, the lot!" he said, his eyes gleaming, as they all walked wearily back home to Belmont Avenue. "But I'm sorry you didn't get a proper go, Ben," Vince said, as they said goodbye. "Tell you what, since you've been such a help, you can come in and use the machines at half-price any time."

****

But though Ben didn't want to avoid Vince any more, it was very hard to get to the studio. He had to spend all Sunday catching up on the homework he hadn't done the day before. All the time he was worrying that he hadn't been able to meet Rory in the virtual coffee shop.

"He must be thinking it was a dream after all," thought Ben. But then, in a way, their whole friendship was a dream. Thinking about this made it impossible to concentrate on his homework which was on the Amazon rainforest and the Second World War.

On Monday at school, everyone was raving about Mister VR's. Ben's popularity rating was high because Vince was his friend and neighbour.

"Lucky!" said Gerry, when Ben let slip that he could play there for half-price.

Ben soon saw that it was going to be difficult to get to the studio on his own. Everyone wanted to go back there after school and it looked as if it would be almost as busy as it had been on Saturday.

In the end, Ben did get some time on a machine, but Dylan was on one side of him and Gerry on the other. They wanted to know what program he had chosen and he had to pretend he was playing 'Alien Invasion'. It wasn't until he saw them swaying and jerking to their own programs that he thought he was safe to go back to 'Virtual Friend'.

Quickly, he called up RORY POLESTAR and the COFFEE SHOP, crossed his fingers in his bulky cyberglove and pressed GO.

Instantly he felt himself sitting at a table looking into a steaming cup of cappuccino. He took a spoonful of froth and chocolate powder and raised it to his lips.

A thump on his back sent Ben's nose into the froth. Even before he looked round, he knew who it was.

"Hey, Bendigo!" said Rory, coming round to sit opposite him. "Well, here we are in the coffee shop. I suppose that makes you Doctor Frankenstein and me some kind of monster."

And, just for once, he wasn't grinning.

Chapter 3
Stuck!

"Rory," said Ben, wiping the froth off his nose. "Am I glad to see you! I couldn't get back on the machines on Saturday. This is the first chance I've had."

"The machines, huh?" said Rory. "So it's true what you told me on the moon."

"Look, I don't know what's true and what's not," said Ben.

And he told Rory everything – Vince's shed, the power cut, Rory's presence at school and how he disappeared.

"So you're saying none of it really happened?" asked Rory. "None of it was real?"

"I don't know," said Ben. "It *felt* real enough." He reached out and touched Rory's sleeve. Of course he could feel it but that didn't prove anything. This was virtual reality.

"If I can come into your world, why can't you come into mine?" asked Rory. "Or maybe, you did. The park was my park. Even this place," he looked around, "could be the *Coffee Bean* on my High Street, but it's all slightly off, just not quite right."

"I'd love to come into your world properly, Rory," said Ben.

"Wait a minute," said Rory, his eyes shining, "I've had an idea."

****

Because of Rory's idea, Ben spent every day after school at Mister VR's. Every evening, after he'd done his homework, he picked his Dad's brains about computer-programming.

By the end of the week, he had run out of pocket money and had spots in front of his eyes.

On Saturday he managed to persuade Vince to let him have a session and pay later. He got to the VR studio early to avoid Dylan and the others and slipped his modified version of 'Virtual Friend' into one of the machines. There was a new settings option now, headed RORY'S HOUSE.

As soon as Ben pressed GO, he found himself in Rory's living room. It was empty but Ben knew where he was from the detailed descriptions Rory had given him, which he had been programming in all week. Ben walked across the room and turned right up the stairs. He could hear the thump of music coming from a room on the first floor.

He didn't knock at the door but just walked in. Rory was sitting on his bed with his eyes closed, moving his head in time to the loud music coming from his stereo.

"Hey, Rory!" said Ben, as cool as could be.

Rory leapt into the air, eyes wide open now. Then he let out a whoop of joy and danced up and down on his bed.

"You did it, Ben! Wicked!"

Ben spent all morning with Rory at his house. They looked in all the rooms and went out into the garden. He met Rory's lovely big Mum and his twin sisters when they got in from shopping and ate homemade cookies.

It was only when Rory's Mum asked Ben to stay to lunch that he realised how late it was. He must have been wearing the helmet and gloves at Mister VR's for hours.

"Thank you, Mrs Polestar," he said, "but I must be getting back." Then he turned to Rory. "Help!" he said. "I'm completely broke and I now owe Vince half of next week's pocket money. I don't know when I'll be able to see you again. Not for a week at least."

"You can't wait that long," said Rory. "You really are in my world. I'll give you some money. When do you think you'll be back?"

"After school on Monday," said Ben.

"See you then," said Rory.

Was it Ben's imagination or was Rory looking more thoughtful than usual?

****

Dad was cross with Ben for being back so late for lunch and started to mutter about his spending too much time and money at Mister VR's. So Ben washed up without being asked and made Dad a cup of coffee before getting out his homework. Luckily it was his favourite subjects this weekend – English, French and I.T.

He wrote an essay about *Lord of the Flies* and then sailed through his computer exercises. After what he had been doing all week it was a piece of cake.

Dad brought him a real piece of cake and a cup of tea, just as he had finished.

"All done, Ben?" he asked. "How about going to the pictures tonight?"

All Ben had left to do was a bit of French so they went to the latest Schwarzenegger film and then had a Chinese takeaway. It was one of their best nights since Mum had died.

Ben got up early on Sunday to do his French homework and then offered to mow the lawn. He was just putting the mower away when Dylan, Gerry, Assad and Kieran called round for him. It was a cold, fine day so they went to kick a football round in the park.

"Didn't see you at Mister VR's yesterday afternoon," said Dylan in a casual voice.

"No," said Ben, dribbling the ball past Assad, "I went in the morning."

"My Mum never lets me go round there till I've done some chores," said Gerry. "It's not fair. It's just because I'm the only girl in the family. I bet you lot don't have to do chores."

"My Mum makes me do my homework on Saturday mornings," said Kieran. "She says she knows I'll leave it to the last minute otherwise."

"Mine's the same," said Assad and Dylan nodded.

Ben didn't say anything. It was at times like this when he really missed his Mum. Dad was great and did a really good job of looking after him but it was hard not being able to join in conversations that began, 'My Mum says...'

He was startled out of his thoughts when Dylan headed the ball at him and said in an even more casual voice, "Come to think of it, we haven't seen much of you all week. What have you been doing?"

Ben couldn't really say he'd been modifying one of Vince's VR programs, especially when Vince didn't know about it himself.

"I've been doing some extra I.T. with Dad," he said, which was true.

"You're so lucky having a Dad in computers," said Kieran. "My Dad sells insurance. How boring is that?"

But Ben could tell that he hadn't fooled Dylan.

****

Monday dragged so slowly Ben thought school would never be over. When it was, he shot out of the gates, clutching the money Rory had given him.

"Hey, wait for us!" shouted Gerry. "We're going to Mister VR's."

"See you there!" Ben shouted back, but he didn't slow down. He ran all the way to Vince's studio and slammed his money down on the reception desk.

He was lucky that Vince always let him put his own program in but he always pretended to use one of the new ones. Now he hurried to start up 'Virtual Friend' as he struggled into his helmet and gloves.

As soon as he was back in Rory's house, Ben started to breathe easily again. They walked round the rooms together, checking the small modifications Ben needed to

make to the program. But there was something strange about Rory. Ben knew him so well that he could tell when something was up. There was something Rory wasn't telling him.

Ben shook his head. First Dylan and now Rory seemed strange – he must be getting paranoid.

"Will you stay for dinner, Ben?" asked Rory's Mum. "I'm making my famous fried chicken."

Ben had just opened his mouth to say 'no thank you', when he had the strangest feeling. All the lights went out and he heard Rory's Mum say, "Oh no, not a power cut in the middle of my cooking!"

Ben's body seemed to swirl and fizz as if he were about to faint. But he didn't. He was still standing in Rory's living room. In the dim light from the window he could see that Rory was giving him that strange look again. And Ben felt different, more solid somehow, even though he hadn't felt *un*solid before.

"You'd better say you'll stay," said Rory.

"Why?" asked Ben, though he had the feeling he knew why. Rory pointed to the dead lights.

"I threw the switch on the fuse box," he said. "I thought it might work the same for you as it did for me when the power went off."

And that was when Ben realised fully that he was not standing in Mister VR's any more.

He was stuck in Rory's real world now.

Chapter 4
No Place Like Home

Ben's Dad knew that Ben was dropping in at Vince's after school so he didn't worry at first. But when suppertime came and went with no sign of Ben, he became anxious. He knocked at Vince's house.

"Have you seen Ben?" he asked.

"Sure I have," said Vince. "He came by the studio after school. Why? Isn't he home yet?"

"No," said Dad, "and that's what's worrying me. Ben is never late without letting me know where he is."

"I wouldn't worry," said Vince. "He's got his head screwed on right, that one. I reckon he's with his school friends. They were in the studio as well. You know, that ginger-haired girl and the three boys he always hangs about with."

Dad was relieved. "Dylan and the others? I've got their phone numbers – I'll give them a ring."

"Good thinking," said Vince. "And let me know what they say. If he's not at one of their houses, I'll help you look for him. But that's where he'll be, mark my words."

But he wasn't. Dad rang all of the other four children's houses and got the same story. Ben had been at Mister VR's when they arrived, already into his virtual reality game, but he had gone by the time they finished theirs.

Dylan seemed quite miffed about it. "Ben didn't even say goodbye to us."

Now Dad was really alarmed. It was getting dark. He called on Vince and they set out with torches, slowly re-tracing the route from Belmont Avenue to the studio in the High Street.

"If we don't find him soon," said Dad, "I'm phoning the police."

****

Ben couldn't really enjoy the fried chicken, even though it was delicious. They ate by candlelight.

"Good job we cook on gas," said Rory's Mum for the umpteenth time. "It was hard work finishing this by the light of a few candles."

"Well worth it though, Mum," said Rory. "Great, isn't it, Ben?"

"Yes, thank you, Mrs Polestar," said Ben. "You're a great cook."

"Thank you, Ben, you're a real gentleman," said Rory's Mum. "You can visit us any time."

Ben and Rory exchanged glances by the flickering candlelight. They were both wondering how long this particular visit would last.

After washing up in the semi-dark kitchen, they went up to Rory's room. Ben was beside himself with worry.

"Why did you switch the power off? My Dad will be going bananas!"

"It's only the same as what happened to me," said Rory.

"But the difference is that you did it to me on purpose. What happened to you was an accident," said Ben.

The two boys were glaring at each other. It was the first time they had had anything like a row.

"Hey, man," said Rory. "Don't let's fight. I'll turn the electricity back on and send you back. I just wanted to see if it would work. Now I've found out it does, we can make you really be here any time."

"OK," said Ben. He remembered that Rory had always been the inventive one, up for any adventure.

"Friends again?" asked Rory.

"Friends again," said Ben and they slapped hands.

They crept down the dark stairs to the cellar.

"Why didn't your Mum just switch the power back on herself?" Ben whispered on the way down.

"She doesn't trust electricity," Rory whispered back. "Thinks it's dangerous stuff. I don't think she even knows where the fusebox is. She's waiting for my Dad to get back from his shift and fix it."

They reached the cellar and Rory went over to the cupboard where the fusebox was kept. He shone a little pocket torch on it and Ben saw the big, white switch. Rory reached over and flipped it down.

"Cheerio, Bendigo!" he said.

****

By now, Dad was fearing the worst. He and Vince had searched all the back streets between home and the High Street and there had been no sign of Ben. It was a cold night and it was getting late so there were very few people of his age still out. People were hurrying home to their warm houses and hot dinners and didn't want to stop and talk.

But Dad went on, asking everyone if they'd seen a shortish, average-looking, twelve-year-old boy. No-one had.

"It's no good, Vince," he said. "We'll have to phone the police."

"Come to the studio, then," said Vince, "if you think you really must. It's closer than home."

****

When Rory threw the switch, Ben closed his eyes, expecting to feel a bit giddy at least. But he didn't.

He opened his eyes. The lights were all back on and Rory was staring at him. They were both still in the cellar.

"Praise be!" they heard Rory's Mum saying upstairs. "The power's back on!"

Perhaps I'm still here but back in the Virtual Reality program, thought Ben. Perhaps I'm really in Mister VR's now? Just like when I got here ...

Ben clutched at his head and hands, trying to take off the helmet and gloves that should have been there, waiting for the jolt back to reality. But all the time, he knew it was useless. He knew that he was as real in Rory's world as Rory had been in his a few months ago.

"I'm sorry, man," said Rory. "Why didn't it work?"

"I don't know," said Ben miserably. "I don't understand why it worked in the first place, this evening or last September. You just went away when the power came back on."

When they were back in his room, Rory sat on the bed and looked thoughtful, "But I wasn't there all the time, you say," he said.

"No," said Ben, trying hard to remember and to blot out the image of Dad worrying about him. "It was as if you were only there when I wanted you. You weren't there when you would have made things difficult. You were around at lunch and breaktimes and after school but never during lessons. Where did you go?"

Rory spread his hands out. "Search me," he said. "That time's all a bit hazy for me. Like when you've had the flu and you can't remember what you've said or done."

"Hang on," said Ben. "Where did you go at night-time, after you left my house?"

Rory shrugged. "Home, I guess."

"Then why can't I?" said Ben. He remembered a film he used to watch with his Mum when he was little. It was about a girl whose house was blown away by a tornado and landed in a magic country. When she wanted to go home, she just had to click her red shoes together. Ben looked down at his grubby trainers and suddenly felt so homesick he thought he was going to cry.

"Thing is, Bendigo," said Rory, "this isn't like science, is it? It's more like magic. Maybe you have to sort of wish to make things happen."

Ben wished as hard as he could but he was still there in Rory's bedroom.

"Let's go out," said Rory. "It's no good staying here. I think better when I'm on the move."

He took his skateboard and called out to his Mum that they were just going out for a bit. Ben could see that Rory was allowed a lot more freedom than he was. Dad would never have let him out so late.

As they walked down Rory's road, Ben started to ask questions about his neighbourhood. They passed a bus stop but Ben didn't recognise any of the numbers on the board. Was Rory's world the same as his, only further away, or were they living in different dimensions?

Of course, why hadn't he thought of it before?

"Who's the Prime Minister?" Ben said suddenly, grabbing Rory by the sleeve.

Rory looked at him as if he'd gone mad.

"Just answer me!" said Ben urgently. "And who won the Cup last year and what's the name of the latest Schwarzenegger film?"

When Ben heard Rory's answers he fell on him laughing.

"This is great!" said Ben. "We live in the same world! Tell me your address properly – and your phone number."

Ben wrote it all down with a stub of pencil on a bus ticket he found in his pocket.

"You don't live very far away from me," said Ben. "I bet I could even take a train home. Though I still wouldn't get there till the middle of the night." He was flooded with relief. Now he could even phone Dad, though goodness knows what he was going to tell him.

"So we can see each other just like ordinary friends?" said Rory. He was grinning at first but then he looked sad. "I liked it better when we were virtual friends. That's more kind of special."

"I've got an idea about that," said Ben. "We'll work on it the next time I can get to you through Mister VR's. Only you'll have to promise never to throw the switch on me again like that."

"Promise," said Rory.

"Right," said Ben. "Now I need a station, a train timetable, a phonebox and a very good story."

****

"Here we are," said Vince. "Cheer up, mate. I'm sure there's a simple explanation. I've never had any kids myself but I used to be one and I was a right little terror when it came to forgetting the time. Used to drive my poor old Mum crazy. Now, hang on a minute, just let me find my keys."

He let them into the darkened studio and switched the lights on. Nothing happened. Vince turned on his torch, sighing.

"That Sylvia. She locked up tonight. Ever since we got cut off that time at home, she's so paranoid about wasting electricity, that I bet she's turned it off at the fusebox. I'll have it on in a jiffy and then you can make your call."

Dad wasn't really listening. He was too worried about Ben to pay attention to anything Vince said. He just slumped into a chair and gazed dully at the circle of torchlight.

Vince went off into the back room, still chattering. "I've never met a woman yet who understands electricity," he was saying. "Sylvia seems to think it just leaks out like gas ..."

All of a sudden, Mister VR's was illuminated by its blindingly bright striplights.

"Ben!" gasped Dad.

And there was Ben standing at one of the machines, in his helmet and goggles, looking as dazed as Dad.

But neither of them was as surprised as Vince, who was coming back into the room. His jaw dropped, his hair seemed to stand on end. He was gasping like a landed fish.

"How on earth did you get here?" Vince said at last.

But by then Ben had seen Dad and wrenched off the virtual reality gear and hurled himself into his arms. They were both talking at once.

"Where have you been ...?"

"I thought you'd be mad ..."

"I asked everyone ..."

But Vince cut in. "That woman must be losing her marbles! How could she have locked up with you still in here?"

Ben thought fast. He hated lying but he couldn't get Sylvia into trouble. "I came over all drowsy," he said, "and I think I must have fallen asleep behind the machine. I only just woke up when all the lights came on." He had his fingers crossed all the time he said it.

Both Vince and Dad looked so relieved that Ben couldn't feel sorry about the lie.

As they all walked home together, Ben felt a warm glow. Somewhere, twenty miles on the other side of town, lived his best friend. But Ben knew how they could be with each other in seconds.

Rory Polestar and Ben Silver were going to go on being virtual friends.

Who is Barrington Stoke?

Barrington Stoke was a famous and much-loved story-teller. He travelled from village to village carrying a lantern to light his way. He arrived as it grew dark and when the young boys and girls of the village saw the glow of his lantern, they hurried to the central meeting place. They were full of excitement and expectation, for his stories were always wonderful.

Then Barrington Stoke set down his lantern. In the flickering light the listeners were enthralled by his tales of adventure, horror and mystery. He knew exactly what they liked best and he loved telling a good story. And another. And then another. When the lantern burned low and dawn was nearly breaking, he slipped away. He was gone by morning, only to appear the next day in some other village to tell the next story.

Barrington Stoke would like to thank all its readers for commenting on the manuscript before publication and in particular:

Tom Begg
Louise Galloway
Luke Holmes
Tara Kay
Victoria Loftus
Brian McLintock
Belinda Martin
Tiara Mohammed
Ben Parkes
Joanna Robertson
Vicky Stewart
Alex Taylor
Holly Ufnowski
Alison Waugh

Become a Consultant!

Would you like to give us feedback on our titles before they are published? Contact us at the email address below – we'd love to hear from you!

Email: info@barringtonstoke.co.uk
Website: www.barringtonstoke.co.uk

If you loved this story, why don't you read ...

The Odd Couple

by Yvonne Coppard

What are your neighbours like? Could they be master criminals? Danny has secretly been watching his neighbours. He is convinced that they are involved in something very fishy. What exactly are they up to? Danny and his friend decide to follow them and find out more ...

Visit our website!
www.barrringtonstoke.co.uk